This book belongs to

Sophia SPARKS

Elanor Best · Lara Ede

make believe ideas

A glance at *Sophia*
will draw your **attention**
to the *bow* that unlocks
her flair for **invention**.

This *bow* is the **key**
to her skill, she is **sure**:
when she **wears** it,
she **thinks** of
inventions galore.

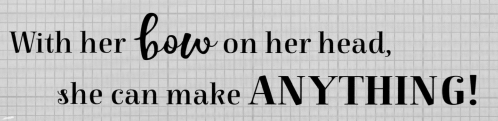

With her *bow* on her head,
she can make ANYTHING!
From glitter-fuelled ROCKETS
with **jet-thruster** springs …

to ROBOTS that dance
as they tie up your laces,

and HOUSES with **legs**
that compete in **sport races**.

But no one invents **different** things like *Sophia.*
Instead, all her friends work on just **one** idea:

Isaac builds
JET-ENGiNES
out of bright steel;

Marie invents
POTIONS;

Marie's Cures

and Nick builds
NEW WHEELS.

One day, the students
were given a **TEST**:

change sign

to **transform**
their old bus
and make it the **best.**

Sophia reached out
for her trustworthy **bow**,
but saw, with **dismay**
it had **vanished** –

"OH, NO!

Mega mallet

Thinking cap

Science shades

Things to do...

Oil dancing robot
Running shoes for house

Twisters and turners

Whizz grippers

Sophia

Nail knocker

Bolt busters

Her stomach: it **churned**.
Her spirits: they **sank**.

She thought,
with no bow,
that her mind would stay
BLANK!

Meanwhile, the others
had worked at such **pace**,
they were **already** bolting
INVENTIONS in place.

But her classmates' IDEAS
weren't working in **sync**,
and **no one** could work out
the **one** *MISSING* link.

"IT'S NO USE,

cried *Sophia*,
as she **stormed** off to lunch . . .
which was when, as it happens,
she had a great **hunch**.

She saw in the **shape**
of the **mash** on her plate
how to blend their IDEAS
and make the bus **GREAT!**

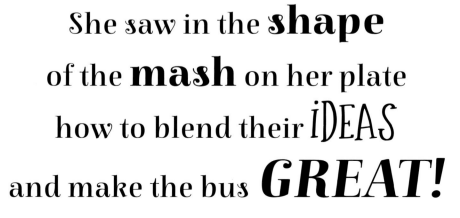

She ran to the lab and, as **quick** as a FLASH,
showed all her friends
the **plan** made of
MASH!

"If we work alone, then we **won**'t get this done.
But **TOGETHER**, we'll do it
and even have
FUN!"

The lab became noisy
with **hammers** and **drills**.
as the LiTTLE INVENTORS
used **ALL** of their skills.

At last, they could see,
when they worked as a **team**,
they could make something
AWESOME...

BOW1

ball pit

COOKIES

cookie
dispenser

slide
exit

rainbow fuel
pump

games room

cinema suite

the bus
of their
DREAMS!

auto-drive panel

jet engine

bouncy wheel

"You've all **PASSED** the test,"
said their teacher with **glee**.

LOCAL
TV | Breaking news : New school bus invented at Little Laboratory School •

"This BUS is so **fun**,
it's made
local TV!"

"You mixed your **inventions** to make every fixture. Well done to *Sophia,* who **saw** the **big picture**."

Whilst all of her CLASSMATES were watching the news, Sophia caught sight of her bow by their SHOES.

She picked it up quickly and said, her voice low,

"My IDEAS are **mine**: they don't come from this *bow!*"

But she tied it in place,
and then gave a **big grin**,
for the *bow* had made her know
her **ideas** were **within**.